THERE WAS AN
OLD GATOR
WHO SWALLOWED
A MOTH

B. J. Lee • Illustrated by David Opie

PELICAN PUBLISHING COMPANY

GRETNA 2019

The word "Pelican" and the depiction of a pelican are trademarks of Pelican Publishing Company, Inc., and are registered in the U.S. Patent and Trademark Office.

Library of Congress Cataloging-in-Publication Data

Names: Lee, B. J. (Poet), author. | Opie, David, illustrator.
Title: There was an old gator who swallowed a moth / by B. J. Lee ;
   illustrated by David Opie.
Description: Gretna : Pelican Publishing Company, 2019. | Summary: In this variation on the
   traditional cumulative rhyme, a crab, an eel, and a manatee are part of the feast for an alligator.
Identifiers: LCCN 2018016167| ISBN 9781455624416 (hardcover : alk. paper) |
   ISBN 9781455624423 (ebook)
Subjects: LCSH: Folk songs, English—Texts. | CYAC: Folk songs. | Nonsense verses.
Classification: LCC PZ8.3.L49917 The 2019 | DDC 782.42 [E]—dc23 LC record available at https://
   lccn.loc.gov/2018016167

Printed in Malaysia
Published by Pelican Publishing Company, Inc.
1000 Burmaster Street, Gretna, Louisiana 70053
www.pelicanpub.com

To my wonderful husband, Malcolm

There was an old gator who swallowed a moth.
I don't know why he swallowed the moth.

It made him cough.

There was an old gator who swallowed a crab
that skittered and scuttled and gave him a jab.
He swallowed the crab to grab the moth.
I don't know why he swallowed the moth.
It made him cough.

There was an old gator who swallowed an eel.
Quite an ordeal, to swallow an eel!
He swallowed the eel to nab the crab
that skittered and scuttled and gave him a jab.

He swallowed the crab to grab the moth.
I don't know why he swallowed the moth.
It made him cough.

There was an old gator who swallowed a ray.
With no delay, he swallowed that ray!

He swallowed the ray to waylay the eel.
He swallowed the eel to nab the crab
that skittered and scuttled and gave him a jab.
He swallowed the crab to grab the moth.
I don't know why he swallowed the moth.
It made him cough.

There was an old gator who swallowed a pelican.
No gator's belly can handle a pelican!
He swallowed the pelican to prey on the ray.
He swallowed the ray to waylay the eel.
He swallowed the eel to nab the crab
that skittered and scuttled and gave him a jab.
He swallowed the crab to grab the moth.
I don't know why he swallowed the moth.
It made him cough.

There was an old gator who swallowed a panther.
It wasn't the answer to swallow a panther!
He swallowed the panther to pounce on the pelican.
He swallowed the pelican to prey on the ray.
He swallowed the ray to waylay the eel.
He swallowed the eel to nab the crab
that skittered and scuttled and gave him a jab.
He swallowed the crab to grab the moth.
I don't know why he swallowed the moth.
It made him cough.

There was an old gator who swallowed a manatee.
He lost his sanity to swallow a manatee!
He swallowed the manatee to pursue the panther.
He swallowed the panther to pounce on the pelican.
He swallowed the pelican to prey on the ray.
He swallowed the ray to waylay the eel.
He swallowed the eel to nab the crab
that skittered and scuttled and gave him a jab.

He swallowed the crab to grab the moth.
I don't know why he swallowed the moth.
It made him cough.

There was an old gator who swallowed a shark.
It was no lark to swallow a shark!
He swallowed the shark to capture the manatee.
He swallowed the manatee to pursue the panther.
He swallowed the panther to pounce on the pelican.
He swallowed the pelican to prey on the ray.
He swallowed the ray to waylay the eel.

He swallowed the eel to nab the crab
that skittered and scuttled and gave him a jab.
He swallowed the crab to grab the moth.
I don't know why he swallowed the moth.
It made him cough.

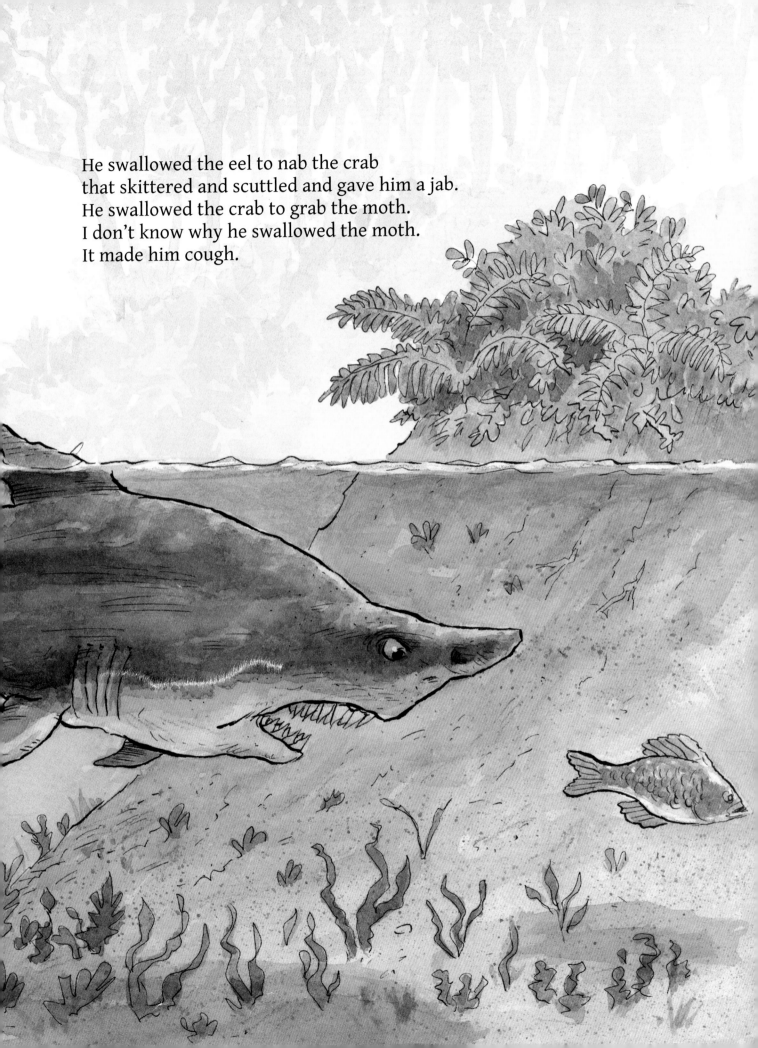

There was an old gator who gulped a lagoon.
What a loon—an entire lagoon!
That gator expanded just like a balloon.

Then the moth he had swallowed made him

COUGH! COUGH! COUGH!

till one final cough carried everything off.

Author's Note

There Was an Old Gator Who Swallowed a Moth is based on the nursery rhyme "There Was an Old Lady Who Swallowed a Fly." Gator lives in a Florida lagoon, where he encounters many Florida animals and can't help but . . . well . . . swallow them! Florida is filled with interesting animals such as the pelican, Florida panther, manatee, ray, shark, and Gator himself, of course. B. J. Lee, poet and author, also lives in Florida, where she has seen her fair share of gators.